the kindness of strangers

BY

sandy woolworth

illustrated by

carol Tippit woolworth

TIPWORTH PRESS

Published by **TIPWORTH PRESS** © 2012 • All rights reserved.

LCCN: 2012939595
ISBN: 978-0-9852645-0-5

ACKNOWLEDGEMENT

I wish to offer my sincerest thanks to Claire Ford for her constant faith, encouragement, reading, re-reading, and editing of this book. Her sharp eyes have kept me in line and for this I am truly grateful.

I also wish to thank Leslie Jamison and her mother, Kathleen Jamison for their editing skills and literary guidance.

A special thanks goes to my wife, Carol, whose story critiques aided me throughout the entire process and whose illustrations brought to life, for all to see, Winnie's unique story.

And there would be no book without Winnie Woolworth, whose plight and bravery inspired me to write this story.

DEDICATION

This book is dedicated to all of the animals of the world,

but especially to those who

go through life encumbered and in pain.

My heart goes out to you.

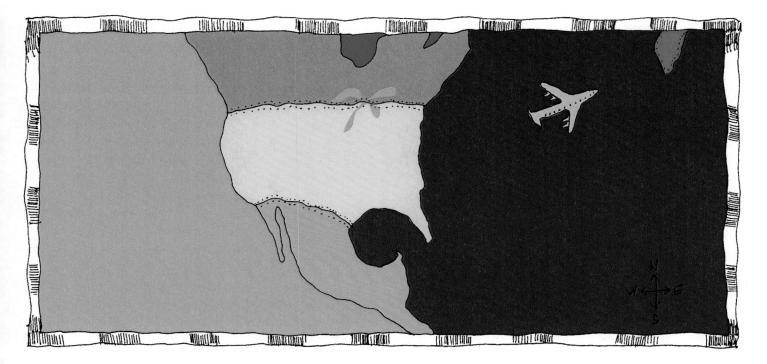

p r o l o g u e

The Atlantic at night is somehow a richer black than the Pacific. It's a blackness that appears to go downward forever. And it seems colder too. Soldiers will tell you that. Soldiers who have been stranded, treading water, waiting. Really anyone will report the difference if they've experienced both. These are, no doubt, unlucky people because to register the nuance of darkness between two bodies of water, you would have to spend considerable time somewhere out of the sight of land. Now this can happen in a perfectly normal way, say if you're a salvage diver doing something illicit under the cloak of night or, perhaps a navy seal, although your wet time would be a lot shorter than that of a strandee, and, of course, you'd be thinking about your task or job, not how dark and cold it is. No, to really know the difference, you'd have to be very unlucky. As unlucky as me.

ARE WE THERE YET?

Focusing on something is not my forte. Focusing for me is what I do the opposite of unless food is involved. But here I am, caught as it were, in an irony of life, focusing on keeping my head above water, trying to keep my mouth closed and my snout up. It's cold, very cold, and I think I'm shivering but can't really tell. The salty water hurts my eyes and has filled my ears. My front legs are beyond tired, paddling anemic, insignificant strokes that are getting slower and shorter.

My left rear leg doesn't function at all because of paralysis from my 12th vertebrae on back, a condition I've lived with for two years now. My right leg still has plenty of kicking power thanks to physical therapy, but this is definitely not physical therapy.

No sleep, nor food, nor drinking water has come my way for a very long time. I am in the Atlantic Ocean somewhere between the United States and England, and my visibility is constantly cut off because of the choppy water. When I can see, my heart sinks because all I see is more water. No place to rest or sleep or dream.

But I'm a dog and 99 percent of me functions on instinct. It doesn't cross my mind to stop "dog paddling".

My undercoat, my last barrier against the cold and damp is now completely saturated. Its ability to insulate is gone, allowing my skin to freeze, causing too much energy to go toward shivering, not paddling.

And the darkness has enveloped not only me, but the entire Atlantic. The black water below seems to be thriving with activity. I can sense other animals beneath me. I haven't actually seen anyone but I'm receiving electrical impulses from other life. This is my territory, but I honestly don't think I could muster a territorial growl. Must keep paddling, must stay awake, must focus!

yesterday...
ROUTINE, SCHMOUTINE

I have very specific needs and likes that I feel must take place at particular times throughout the day. Corgis are punctual and you'd better be too! So at 5:20AM I like to get things started around here toward my immediate goal by "boofing." Boofing is my word for little semi-silent barks that alert Francine Dumont, my primary master, that it's time to carry me (because of my paralysis) to the kitchen. I've named them a boof because of what they do to my flaps (or lips in human terms). A boof is a very muffled, discrete bark done by not opening one's snout while barking. When this occurs, the air expelled puffs out one's flaps and the ever so pleasant boof sound is emitted. I feel that boofing is an appropriately gentle wake-up call to my so deserving primaries, Francine and Reynaldo. So once Francine, and sometimes Reynaldo, are boofed awake, and we've made it to the kitchen, my goal has been attained, it's outdoor time.

After a quick utility walk I am pretty patient about when my breakfast will be served. At the beginning of each week Francine cooks up a delicious batch of chicken or ground beef, beans, carrots, buttermilk or

 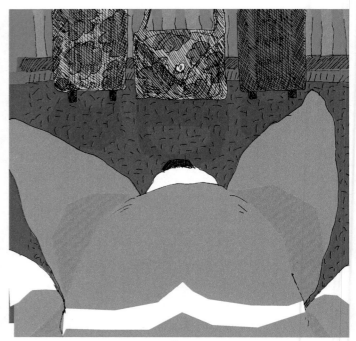

yogurt, beets and barley, enough to last a week. I really enjoy this meal, though it could use something dead from the back yard.

　　While I eat, Francine grinds coffee and prepares it (not for me), but the overwhelming aroma, so complete from a dog's point of view, enhances my chomping pleasure. It is usually at this point, around 6:30AM that Reynaldo comes down, and they drink coffee and read the paper and talk. The radio is telling them the news and they're chatting away creating a warm friendly backdrop of safe human sounds. It's all very pleasant.

　　At 7AM sharp Francine puts me in my wheelchair and the two of us go for a walk in the neighborhood. We meet Lyn, who usually sings a little Irish ditty to me; Mark, with his head buried in his book while walking with

Archie; Claire and her three beagles, Jackson, Winston, and Lundsford; Arlene with that little mixed breed Corgi, Cliffy Jo; and other neighbors whose names I'm vague on. One neighbor I'm not vague on, Bob, always has a milk bone at the ready for me, causing his own two golden retrievers unparalleled jealousy. After the walk I'm lifted out of my "chair" and Francine takes me to her painting studio in the basement. I lie under her feet as she paints, bringing us to about 9AM, sometimes 10.

　　When "painting" is done, we go upstairs to the office. Here my place is under her desk where she, and Reynaldo, work on what they call graphic design. This is another comfort zone for me with much talking and laughing between the two of them. They never forget me, taking time out to rough-up my skin or give me a few

pats on the head. This goes on until around noon. I'm not in control at this point as my boofing has no effect, and there's nothing I would change anyway. This is just the way things are everyday.

Sometimes at noon they leave the house, and leave me alone. I sleep and dream of running and finding food or of dominating other dogs. When they come back we all settle into our respective spots and play our roles.

My afternoon walk, at around 3PM, brings us in contact with another group of people such as Karen and her new puppy, Cooper. Or Dave, Jerry and Lohey, a nervous canine who, I think, is in love with me. By 3:30PM we're back and I get a treat; a carrot. The carrot is an unbelievably perfect food, my favorite food. I positively love it. It's easy to grasp and has a great crunch

to it. From my point of view it's like having the ever forbidden chicken bone, also perfect, crunchy, and flavorful, but apparently dangerous to my esophagus.

Now it's time to sleep and dream some more. I never had puppies but I often dream about them. In a puppy dream I get covered in warm, squeaking little furry bodies tumbling everywhere around me and I'm all warm and happy and, of course, there's food everywhere.

Five o'clock arrives and we are all in the kitchen. Francine and Reynaldo each get a beer and I get a bowl of dinner. While I'm eating, Francine makes dinner for the two of them, they eat at a much more leisurely pace than I ever would, and then Reynaldo washes the dishes.

7PM and time for my final walk. This is a big one because everyone is out either walking their dogs or sitting on their porch. The conversations are pretty long and everyone is having a good time. To support myself on my two front legs the whole time because of my wheelchair is tiring, but I get a lot of attention and some treats, so it's worth it.

When 8:30PM arrives, we are home and in the bedroom. Francine massages my back legs, combs me, and it's simply wonderful. The TV is on and they watch a movie, then read as I sleep and dream.

At about 11PM, lights out and everyone is asleep. It's dark and womblike, and I sleep deeply, dreaming till 5:20AM.

There's somethin' Happenin' Here

As you can see I have a rather steady, routine-oriented life and my breed, Corgi, needs and loves routine more than anything. So you will understand how awful it was one morning in August when I didn't get to use my fabulous, patented and copyrighted boof to wake anyone up. They were already awake; the bed was made; showers were being taken; and things out of the ordinary were taking place. For example, they had suitcases on the bed and clothes were everywhere.

I was finally taken down to the kitchen, given my breakfast and then hurriedly taken for a walk, but only a utility walk, no treats or socializing, then back to the house.

Once there, I was placed into my travel crate and then into the back of the station wagon along with two suitcases. We drove along my walk route and then into uncharted territory at a pretty fast pace.

In about half an hour we arrived at AIRPORT PARKING. I couldn't actually figure this out, but I knew I wasn't comfortable with it.

We left the car, and my crate was placed on wheels and rolled to a counter where I was taken out of my crate and placed in a slightly larger one. The wheelchair was attached to Reynaldo's suitcase so there was no chance of mobility. I rolled over onto my side and waited. I didn't know what was going on but Francine slipped me two,

slightly bitter carrots that made me amazingly happy.

Next thing I knew, my new crate and I were on a conveyor belt on our way out to the tarmac. This was a totally new sensation for me but I wasn't able to take it in the way I normally would because of a cloud of drowsiness enveloping my senses. In a desperate attempt to right myself before I fell asleep, I banged my snout on the grillwork of the crate's door, which stung me awake for a few seconds and gave me enough adrenaline to get onto my stomach for what I assumed would be a proper sleep. Drowsiness was certainly making my eyelids heavy, but with so much jostling I remained awake and alert.

Reynaldo and Francine were nowhere in sight and within seconds I was going up high and into the belly of the airplane. My crate was placed on top of another one just like it with an animal inside. Across from me was one more, possibly larger. I wasn't able to see who was in it and there were so many smells that I couldn't get a handle on any one particular odor. The man who did the crate work looked inside at me and said something friendly. He then secured my new home to the wall of the plane and left we three living, breathing types all alone in this dark, strange place. And then, with one eye barely open and the other completely closed, I drifted off.

TAKING FLIGHT

Oh my! So drowsy, I can barely lift my head. But something is happening and I had better be alert for it. That something is the airplane taking off and it feels very strange to me. I'm sliding to the back of my slippery crate, and I'm not able to move on my own at all. There's a lot of pressure. Things are shifting and moving around in the airplane's hold and it's incredibly scary. Suddenly there's an abrupt change in the pressure and I feel as though I'm floating and sliding more to the front of the crate.

Finally, and thankfully, things have settled down. We've leveled off and I'm able to move to the center of my crate. That was terrible and I don't want to go through that ever again. I have no idea of what just took place but it certainly defied all of the laws of a Corgi's perfect order. And being a Corgi, a dog, the memory of the recent excitement is fading, allowing me to sleep and dream some more, and it's feeling as though my reoccurring Gus dream is coming on.

DOES NOT COMPUTE

My Gus dream follows a similar pattern each time. I'm visiting Gus who is a large Saint Bernard. We tolerate each other well. I growl magnificently at him and he responds perfectly by cowering. It's so great because he's so big and I'm sometimes perceived as little.

I love the power of the growl. With it I have complete control and, not oddly because we live in the canine world, we both love these power tussles. I know Gus and dream about him because we share a role in a science project as test subjects and are together a lot.

Gus belongs to Laya and Lord David Northridge. Laya is one of Francine's painting models and Lord David is a neuroscientist. He and Reynaldo talk a lot about a project on which both Reynaldo and Lord David have been working called DOGSPEAK*.

DOGSPEAK has become something of a sensation in the world of neuroscience. Lord David has been connecting Gus and me to a computer by way of a stereotactic cap with surface electrodes on the inside and cables running out of it. I would usually mind this, but because I get a tremendous amount of treats during these sessions, I don't. The electrodes don't hurt and because of my lack of mobility I'm turning out to be a much better subject than Gus, who always shakes off the electrodes during the experiments and walks away. As strange as this may sound, I have no idea what this is for, but you are actually reading the results of DOGSPEAK's transcribed retrievals.

DOGSPEAK is a totally human concept and does not "compute" in the animal world at all. But here's what my brain has understood it to be. As the electrodes gather and relay my brain's impulses, the program makes a story out of them. These stories are created by the use of algorithms. It won't produce speech, just the written word.

I, as a dog, smell, see, hear, feel and taste tremendous amounts of stimuli. It all goes into my brain. And being a dog, I simply act on what is taken in (or not act, as the case may be). DOGSPEAK, on the other hand, puts together the obvious scenarios attached to the combination of all my senses, but especially smelling, hearing and seeing.

It's interesting that DOGSPEAK won't allow me to understand questions. It doesn't translate human into dog. Maybe if Reynaldo or Lord David put electrodes on their heads it would work, but that will never happen.

As DOGSPEAK has gotten out there in the world of research, scientists are finding it not to be uncommon for dogs in particular to exhibit a syndrome not unlike Tourette's. A certain type of barking is actually the expression of the unmentionable.

Another discovery, and here the name of the program should really be ANIMALSPEAK not DOGSPEAK, is that it will work for all animals except, of course, parrots.

* See page 48 for more information

13

PRIMARY CARE

Francine is my primary. I say this because, for example, when it's time to go outside and we are in the kitchen, it's Francine, not Reynaldo, who lifts me up into her arms like a little baby and places me into my wheelchair. I love this for two reasons. One, she makes a lot of cute sounds which excite me and make me happy; and two, I'm able to see if there is any food on the countertops or in the sink. Just the sight of food drives me wild. I have hope when I see food. I'm hoping some mistake or accident will happen and I'll end up with food. Please notice my use of the word food. I really don't care what form the food takes, anything edible is all that's required here.

Another example: when we are out on the street, Francine is very patient with me. As a compromised canine, I walk very slowly, but she doesn't mind at all. She'll let me stand still for a while to sniff to my heart's content, or sometimes pick something to eat off the street, which prompts only the slightest of reprimands. If I'm sick in the house, it's Francine to the rescue. Reynaldo, who loves me, is my secondary because he doesn't do the hands-on, twenty four-seven maintenance that Francine does.

And here's something she does that is really special. At night, after my last walk, Francine takes each back leg and massages it with her fingers. She also takes my wrists, (yes, we have wrists) and gently bends my paws back and forth to keep them from seizing. It feels exceptionally spendid. And she usually rubs my neck too.

Then, after massage, it's a complete and thorough combing out. She rolls me over on my back and works on all of the under hair on my chest and belly. Amazingly, it will all grow back overnight. I close my eyes when she does this, and my mind goes blank with bliss.

DOG IS MY CO-PILOT

When the plane crashed I was still asleep, but because I was upside down and choking, I abruptly awoke. My crate was mercifully open, floating in the water, but not for long. The surrounding seascape was a mess of suitcases, airplane seats, airplane pieces, food, two other animal crates and people, lots of people.

Busy with the task of getting right side up in order to achieve some sort of floating equilibrium, I was finally able to sense the absence of Francine and Reynaldo, and the presence of many strangers.

Smelling blood and seeing the large white airplane's body broken in half with people flailing in and around it, fire everywhere, I think I developed a little anxiety. In the two animal crates I traveled with were large motionless dogs, and I didn't sense any electricity from them.

Running on "autocorgi," fueled by fear and moving away now, my feet were frantically paddling under me (except of course my left rear leg), blindly moving me away, but to where?

With all senses intensely saturated and confusion setting in,

only faintly did I think I heard Reynaldo calling out for Francine and perhaps yelling, "Winnie". It was such a new and awful experience, not the way things are supposed to be. Or more literally, not what I had been accustomed to. But then again, maybe things are supposed to be this way.

I sensed everyone's fright, which naturally frightened me.

The screaming and crying made me so worried, so sad. I'd never seen humans behave this way! I depend on humans, specifically my primaries, to behave in certain, predictable ways such as standing and/or walking, or sitting, talking, laughing, or staring at something, but flailing arms and screaming heads…I didn't know what to think or how to react. Would I ever see Francine and Reynaldo again? And my world, THE WORLD, what has happened to it?

Paddling as fast as I could while compensating for my propensity to travel in a leftward circle brought me close to someone smashing the water with his hand. His mindless hitting of the water, though understandable because he was missing his other arm,

17

concerned me greatly since he might hit me, pushing me under, which would be a disaster. I can't go under. There's no energy reserve for going under, for getting back up, gasping for air, and then continuing on my way. So I paddled even harder than before, with my legs going crazy and beginning to cramp, just to put a little distance between me and this sad but dangerous human, when suddenly he stopped moving and all was silent in our little, shared piece of the Atlantic.

The fire had moved all over the plane. The people remaining inside were jumping out into the cold, choppy water to douse their flames. Still no sign of Francine or Reynaldo, but I may have heard Reynaldo's voice again. The bitter smoke knocked out my sense of smell, my main sense, and though sight and sound were vivid and loud, I was, for the most part, helpless.

The fire tired of the plane and slid off to blanket the water. Its plan was to move quickly my way, searing my wet fur. The resulting heat was too hot to stay there so I made another grand paddling effort to distance myself from that boiling, steaming place.

During the grand paddle I heard a scary noise from above and felt a great deal of wind. Two helicopters were hovering overhead. The coil of air they created moved the fire away from me. Good for them, but it was also pushing me down into the water. Nothing could float under those circumstances and consequently, I was forced under the surface, unable to breath. I could see, through the water, people on a rope going up into the helicopters. I saw Reynaldo alone. There was no Francine. I barked and choked while underwater but, of course, he didn't hear me.

Nearly blacking out from

holding my breath and then using said breath for that stupid attempt at a bark, I had to get to the surface quickly. Paddling hard to get my snout above the surface, the wind kept me under, until, for no apparent reason that I could see, the helicopters moved to the other side of the plane and then farther and farther away.

With the wind gone I popped up to the surface immediately. I gulped air, water, and fuel all at the same time. I couldn't stop choking and I kept going under. Each dunking caused my legs to paddle up to the surface at lightning speed to get a little bit of air in my lungs and after many dunks air replaced the water there.

I could now settle down a little bit and take in my surroundings. There was no evidence of the airplane, no more helicopters, a lot of floating suitcases, seats, the two dog crates

18

(but not mine) and many, many people bobbing lifelessly in the choppy, cold water.

I could also see that no one was coming for me. I've never been this alone or this sad in my entire life. I'm used to people helping me, but there were no people now. I was truly alone and actually whimpering, which, even with my arthritis and paralysis, I've rarely done. I was whimpering because, either dead or saved, everyone had been taken care of except me, I've been forgotten.

JUST A WEE DIP IN THE OCEAN

This endless water, this endless trying to stay afloat, angling my head to keep my snout up is wearing me down. When the plane crashed into the Atlantic it was daytime and remained light for a few hours. It has now been about the same amount of time in the dark.

I'm not paddling any more, my short front legs will not move, so I drift, and now my nose is bumping into something. A large, white, flat, crunchy something with seemingly no weight to it. I'm going to attempt to climb onto it, and this is taking everything I have because I'm using my snout to shove the thing under me. My method is working, but the hard part is getting my front paws in position to sink my claws into it. I need to do this so I can hold it steady and drag myself onto it. The buoyancy is unbelievable and it keeps popping out from under my snout and away from me. I can just barely paddle toward it to try all over again. On my third try my right paw digs in and really holds it steady. The water is very choppy and my claw hold will be good for only a few seconds but I'm able to bring my other leg into position and now I have a good "toe" hold. I'm water logged and feel twice my regular weight. Pulling myself up is next to impossible but this is my only chance. I can see that the choppy little waves that keep attacking this thing will soon loosen my grip and then I'll be drifting until I sink, so I have to make this happen. With everything I have left I pull myself up. It is almost halfway under me, enough of a platform for me to roll onto my back and slide into the

center of what turns out to be quite a large piece of a packing crate.

I stay on my back and look up for the first time in hours. I see millions of little white dots in a deep black sky. I feel my legs twitching and cramping but I ignore the pain. I don't have to paddle anymore and I'm out of the water.

PECKING ORDER

It's daylight and I've been dreaming of Francine and breakfast. In my dream everything happens as it normally would except Shorty is there. He's barking at Francine in his most urgent high-pitched tenor bark to let her know that he wants his food RIGHT NOW! I'm frantically running around the island in the kitchen getting to a better vantage point so I can see the food actually go into our bowls in order to be the first to eat.

Did I say I'm running? I told you it was a dream. Now I'm waking up and feel awful. The sun is blindingly white and very hot. Though my sunny side up is completely dry, my down side is soaking wet from the brine of salt water and blood that makes up my styrofoam mattress.

An overwhelming thirst has me craving water more than food, which is a first. Every muscle aches and this arthritis, (didn't I tell you? severe in my hips), is throbbing.

Before I passed out last night I heard the rusty hinge sound of birds conversing. Large, white birds and many of them. Their screeching was somewhat of a comfort because of my fear and loneliness, so I went to sleep to their music. But the morning sun has brought an end to my loneliness.

Five of them have landed on the packing crate I'm floating on and are pecking at me! They jab their beaks into my side, clamp down and twist to try to pull some flesh away. Lying on my left side allows me to kick with my right back leg and my right front. I also try to bite them, but they are very quick. I wish we were at a standoff, but the brine I'm marinating in is turning redder. I don't think I went to sleep to their music, I think I passed out from exhaustion because I'm bleeding all over and a lot of fur is missing. I'm too feeble to keep this up much longer and the birds are full of energy.

On one of my bird bite expeditions I raised my head high enough to peer over the choppy water and sighted land. I couldn't tell how far away it was or how much longer I'd be out here but the wind was picking up and the drift seemed to be toward land.

If my growling weren't so insipid, and if my bites would connect, maybe the birds would go away. But the reality is I'm going to pass out again. I can't wait.

TIME TO WAKE UP

I'm slowly gaining consciousness. I can hear but not see. I can't even move my head or body, but I hear people around me. Young people (by their high voices) and a lot of them, and I smell something. It's fresh water. Someone has put a bowl of water near my mouth and snout, which, crusty with dried salt water and my blood and is partially sealed shut.

They're lifting my head a little and it hurts, but they are getting me into position to drink. A kind soul has inserted a finger into my flaps (lips to you) lifting them to help me open my mouth so my tongue can lap a little water.

Ahh! Fresh water is pouring all over me allowing my eyelids to loosen up. I get one eye a little open and the first thing I notice is there are no more birds. You can imagine what a relief that is. I had thought upon passing out that last time that unconsciousness would last forever. But, as it turned out, I seem to have

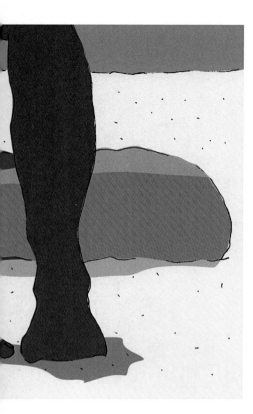

been much closer to land than I thought.

I don't know how my landing happened but here I am on a beach with a lot of excited kids. I don't really have a picture in my mind as to what I look like even on a good day, but a description of me the next day in one of the tabloids said that on this day I was as near to death as a being can be. The paper went on to describe how my fur was entirely pecked away on my right side and my skin was a mass of blood and open wounds. My face was caked with dried blood and I was barely breathing, lying on the packing crate I had ridden on for so long.

I am Winnie, but the tabloids are calling me OCEANDOG. Right now though, none of that tabloid business has happened. I'm still at the drinking-water-for-the-first-time-in-50-hours stage. It's making me gag a little but I'm so thirsty I just don't care.

These people don't know about my paralysis or about Francine and Reynaldo. They do know the airplane I was in went down in the Atlantic off the southern coast of England. I drifted to Brighton Beach and have landed on a stretch of sand in front of the house in which Sir Lawrence Olivier once lived.

I can see more people coming down the beach from my right side. They look to be much larger people, like Reynaldo and Francine's size. People are all over the place now. Lots of picture taking with cameras and cell phones. I love people and I am so happy to be among them again, but how could they not recognize that I need food NOW! I'm a dog and as far as I know, it's people's job to feed dogs, at least that's the way it works in my house. How could they miss that? There is no sign of food anywhere and I am ravenous.

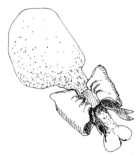

A STAR IS BORN

To be the subject of the day in the British tabloids is no honor. If you want the truth of any news event look elsewhere. I am simply a dog, but if you go by what they are saying about me, I am a superhero named OCEANDOG. OCEANDOG battled sharks, saved a drowning crash victim, swam three-legged for six miles (partly true) and killed numerous seagulls. All of this attention meant nothing to me. Only food, vet care, food, water, some more food, and comfortable sleep (plus some companionship) were meaningful during those first few days.

From the beach I was finally taken to Brightdays Veterinary Hospital headed by Dr. Kevin Cougar. He was the perfect person to take care of me because he wanted none of the media or well wishers' attention which I found a little frightening and confusing. His extreme discretion may have something to do with the fact that Dr. Cougar is the veterinarian for Queen Elizabeth's Corgis, Dorgies, and Labrador retrievers.

He's a very clever, very intuitive vet and proved it by diagnosing my need for food immediately. Though it was of the canned variety, food never tasted as good as that first bite that Dr. Cougar administered by spoon while I was still on my side. Yes, he and Nurse Robin gave me water and hooked me up to something for more liquid to get inside me, but the food was the only thing I was interested in.

My wounds were definitely another story. Not to bore you with my medical milestones, but the blood loss was severe. The entire right side from my shank to my ear had been pecked free of fur. The actual loss of skin was minimal, but one wound caused a tremendous loss of blood. Word went out in the tabloids that OCEANDOG needed a transfusion and people, yes people, offered their own blood. That mania for OCEANDOG lasted for the entire time I was in the hospital and usually, in front of Brightdays, there were 15 to 20 people hanging around hoping to catch a glimpse of OCEANDOG (me), Nurse Robin, or Dr. Cougar. People brought food, toys, and flowers, if you can imagine, as offerings to the "TOP CORGI" as I am being referred to. Headlines such as TOP CORGI WALKS! Or OCEANDOG SITS UP AND OFFERS PAW TO COUGAR! were some of the more ridiculous examples.

Newspapers hold no interest for me except, of course, they remind me of when I was a puppy.

BOW WOW!

When I was presented to Queen Elizabeth, I was looking and feeling quite good even though my entire right side had a large white bandage on it. Emma, Holly and Willow (three of the Queen's Corgis) were with her, as were many people including men and women with really big cameras.

Dr. Cougar provided me with a wheelchair that was pretty good. It lacked the underbelly support I need to keep from dipping mid-spine but otherwise was a first class piece of machinery. He was also responsible for placing me with Her Majesty as he is the royal veterinarian.

The Queen was beaming at me. I felt extreme pleasure in her company and she kept the treats coming (from the pockets in her loden green duffle coat) for all four of us.

At 12 years old and with all that has happened to me, I take everything in stride and so all of the noise and hoopla from the crowd and press didn't bother me. I couldn't help but miss Francine and Reynaldo and wonder where they were, but other than that dark cloud over my head the day was incredible.

Queen Elizabth's house was huge. I stayed in the house with the other Corgis and Dorgis (half Corgi, half Dachshund) for the night. There are nine royal K-9s all together, but some of my growling made it so that only Emma, Holly, Willow and Monty were in the same room

with me. I growled at Vulcan, a Dorgi, who growled back much more forcibly than I, which meant we had to be separated, and I also growled at Monty, a Corgi, with much better results.

Monty reminds me of Shorty, because like Shorty, he and I established a little game. Monty knows I will attack him so he provokes me by looking at me a certain way. I respond by racing toward him and biting him on the ear. This last time I drew blood and Monty whimpered. It was incredibly great and I was elated. Even the Queen could see I played the game really well.

The person who actually takes care of the Queen's dogs is Simon Pearson. He does have a certain way with each of us and he trained all of the Queen's dogs in obedience. Even Vulcan looks up to Simon. He didn't take long to figure me out. He saw right away that I will do anything for food. But the actual feeding is done by the Queen herself, (with Simon taking pictures) at least while I was there. Each of her dogs has a special "royal" bowl and the food is pleasant, if a little uninteresting.

What's fun is that the bowl next to my "guest" bowl is Willow's. Willow eats like Shorty. She noses her food out of the bowl onto the floor and eats from there. Of course much of her food goes into my territory and I grab it without her ever noticing.

I like this situation very much but I don't know how long it will last. I am not secure. I always feel as if some

grand change in my circumstance is about to happen. I'm not part of any pack. Everything since the plane crash has made me feel slightly anxious all the time. My routine no longer exists and why aren't Francine and Reynaldo here?

After dinner the four of us went to the Queen's kennel with the other dogs to sleep. I noticed a bunch of Labradors there but I got no notice from them. The rest of the dogs sleep in a large room and take their cues from Vulcan.

I was placed in a crate, one larger than the one on the airplane, and I didn't mind being in it. It was made of wood and had carved dogs of every breed all over it. Inside it was divided into two sections. The first part, upon entering, had a hard, smooth, cold surface and the other half was of a plush, padded, mattress. My wounds demanded—and frankly my preference in any circumstance would be for—the hard, cold flooring near the front. This gave me a good view of my surroundings and a certain dog. I kept my eye on Vulcan until I slept. Tonight's dream; Francine combing my belly.

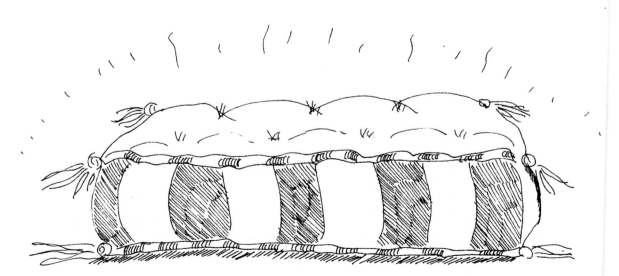

DOG GONE

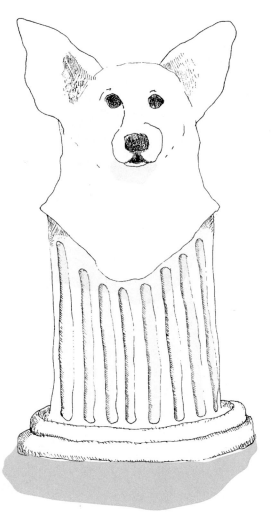

The incidents I have related to you are, as you know, DOGSPEAK's retrieval elaborations on my thoughts and memories. The thoroughness of DOGSPEAK's interpretation of me is beyond reproach. But I want to point out a reality that is not evident in these chapters: a dog's philosophical bent, or just plain dog essence. I will only speak for myself, but please consider that this could be true for the entire animal world (excepting primates).

As a dog I don't think in terms of a future. I don't have vanity or a self-image. I have no expectations. What I have are immediate needs that exist moment to moment. When I'm hungry I crave food and I salivate to a vague stimulating memory of what food (especially Francine's) is like. But I'm not picturing it or reliving the texture, flavor or smell of the food. That craving exists from now to the next now and that last now is forgotten. When I finally do eat, it's now eat, then the next now eat. Each bite, each swallow has its own complete lifetime.

You as a human have certain expectations of the norm that I do not possess. You assume normality to mean good health, shelter, food, companionship, offspring, and a future full of hopes, improved self-image, a lifespan and death.

I, on the other hand, do not think that way at all. When I became paralyzed I perceived this to be part of my normal life. When the plane crashed, I thought this is what happens to everyone (unpleasant though it may be). When I was found on Brighton Beach in England I again thought this is the way it is. Even though I see dogs and people around me all the time with different situations, I only think of my momentary personal existence. When Shorty disappeared I didn't think he ended as a being, I thought he's somewhere else, not within my territory. The same for Francine. Her absence left an ache in my emotional thinking for a long time, but, frankly, other than a slight twinkle in the brain when her name is mentioned, I don't think I remember her at all now. I wish dogs and other animals were more than just "as per the moment" beings, but we're not, only people are.

VULCANIZATION

Queen Elizabeth's love and respect for her dogs is evidenced by the kennel in which they reside. The kennel is actually a huge room in Barkingham Palace. Excuse me, did I say Barkingham? I meant, of course, Buckingham, but if you were to spend any time at all there you'd say Barkingham was right on the mark. The noise level can get pretty intense. We K-9s don't care that much about noise per se, but there are limits. The Queen's Labrador Retrievers are the loudest. But one bark stands out amongst all the others: Vulcan's.

Vulcan is a Dorgi. A breed reportedly invented by the Queen. A breed combining the romance between some misguided Corgi and a lowly Dachshund. I hope my feelings about this are clear. Vulcan is also the most dominant, intimidating alpha male I have ever encountered. He's not overtly vicious, I've never seen him lift a flap or bare a tooth at any of us in the kennel, and he is not big, but he is imposing. If he feels the need to let you know who's boss around here he runs up to you face-to-face, nose-to-nose I should say, and looks through your eyes and out the back of your head. Believe me, you get the message. Stop whatever you are doing and await further instructions or you will...what? Die? We don't really know about death, we dogs just know

comfort/discomfort, yes/no, good/bad, pain/no-pain, and Vulcan's persona says it all.

Vulcan is jet black. His fur is short and smooth to his skin. His ears are overly large, erect, and furry with white insets and he has a long, black, dachshund's tail. He sports a stubborn and imperial bearing, and so I am amused by the relationship he has with Simon Pearson.

Simon is the ultimate alpha. When he's around we are all gratefully submissive to him, even Vulcan. To see Vulcan follow Simon around the kennel wouldn't normally appear strange. In the world of dog packs that's the way it's supposed to be. I know because I was the alpha dog to Shorty, Francine, and Reynaldo. And I'm sure I was the alpha animal to whoever was swimming under me in the Atlantic. But Vulcan has so much alpha-charged electricity pouring out of his fur that I can't help but stare at him with the tiniest bit of, hmmm let's see, is it contempt?

This doesn't go unnoticed by Vulcan. And though I have gotten along with each and every kennel mate in varying degrees for the three nights I've been here, with my crate door now left open so I can come and go as I please (hah, with no wheelchair, fat chance), I have a feeling a showdown is coming.

M . A . D .
(MUTUAL ASSURED DESTRUCTION)

I am outside Buckingham Palace in the enclosed dog "play" area. But play is not what happens out here. This is our bathroom time and more importantly, our chance-to-be-a-dog time. Willow and I are sniffing around in the grass, catching the scent of a couple of male Labs that were out here earlier this morning. We have no fear of the Labs at all. Compared to we Corgis and Dorgis the Labs are laughably inconsequential. They seem to be from another world completely.

We are inching our way along a row of shrubbery, concentrating on capturing a scent that is a little farther up the line of bushes, when who should appear within my radar but Vulcan, and as soon as I see him I know the scene is definitely set, because I've been here before, with Shorty. This scene is so common amongst dogs that it's cliché.

Here's what always used to happen with Shorty. I would be somewhere — bedroom, kitchen, etc. — and he would walk in. We would exchange eye contact. His first mistake! Next, he would stupidly walk by me. Second mistake! He would walk just out of range of my big, biting, snarling, tooth-filled mouth and I would only have to lunge and bite, which I did with such regularity that Francine and Reynaldo would issue only the slightest of reprimands, and that would be for drawing blood. You see this was something both Shorty and I had to do.

We had no choice. I'm dominant and he's not. It's DNA all the way. I have an over abundance of the dominant stuff, as my litter-mates can attest to. I've always been subservient to humans but never to dogs or other animals for that matter.

Getting back to Vulcan, there he is in all his pack leader glory sensing something a little different from this newcomer. He is quite a way down the yard and has just marked an area, all the while keeping his eye on me. Eye contact. Big mistake. I am in my wheelchair but do you think this makes any difference? I don't really know I'm in my wheelchair, all I know is that when Vulcan gets in range, and believe me he can't help himself, he is going to get attacked with such ferocity that I'm not sure I'll even remember what I did. And the thing is, with that eye contact we made, all the signals had been sent and our roles were set in stone.

Now as you may remember, I have a big white cloth bandage on my right side. Every movement I make causes some pain there. Sometimes I even reopen my bird wounds. But this fact will not stop me.

OK, here he comes, and fast. He's doing the only thing he can do in this situation. We are about to be nose-to-nose in a few seconds. I'm watching his Dorgi head get bigger and bigger, closer, closer, NOW! My mouth opens wide, CHOMP, CHOMP, and really loud,

obscene growling from little old me, and that satisfying taste of blood all over my tongue. Vulcan yelps and leaps back in confusion. But he's got a hefty dose of the dominant DNA too, so here comes the counter-attack and it is powerful.

He has come around to my right side and somewhere behind my right ear he CHOMPS, and hard.

The pain startles me but not as much as the fact that he counter-attacked. Shorty never did! This is new to me, perplexing, as a matter of fact. My feelings are really mixed up now and I'm thinking: would it be nice to be dominated by Vulcan, or would I feel more "me" to be the dominant one? There is a delicate balancing point in one's thought processes that guides just about all of our decisions, the left or right, good or bad choices that we constantly make to get through the day, and, here, Vulcan had provided me with a huge one.

Well, it turns out that the "more me" choice won and so I continue the attack. Vulcan is biting my neck behind my right ear so I have to contort my body, which is constrained by my wheelchair, into as much of a "C" shape as possible, allowing me to bite his left side in the ribs, which I do with alacrity.

Vulcan retreats, dripping my blood from his mouth and his blood from his ribcage. I keep snarling and what I'll call attack barking (really piercing, high-pitched short barks) and hold my ground, ready for another attack. During this momentary lull I see Simon running toward us. He's not saying a word, just runs over and scoops up Vulcan (which totally emasculates him) and carries him away.

A few minutes later both Simon and the Queen are kneeling down, checking my bandage, which is partially off. My state of mind right now is indescribably wonderful. I am top dog. I have won. And, to tell you the truth, I can't remember why I feel so great right now. The fight is not even a distant memory and I'll only know who Vulcan is if I see him again. Right now, aside from feeling this exhilaration, I'm completely concentrating on the attention I'm getting from Simon and the Queen.

In only 10 to 15 minutes from whatever happened, Dr. Cougar and Nurse Robin show up to tend to my new wound behind my ear (another bandage) and my side wounds from the birds that have opened up. I guess I would have to say, looking back as far as I'm capable of looking back, this was just an incredible day.

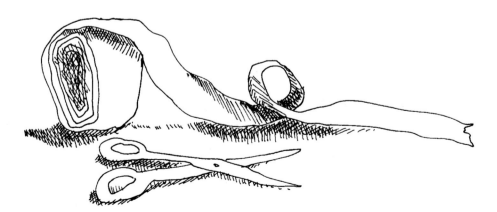

THE WAY BACK

The trip back, from all outward appearances, was un-eventful. If you were to hover above the Queen Mary 2 and then dive into the bowels of the ship to where our cabin was located, you would observe a state of event surprising, but given a little thought, not unexpected.

My painful, but charmed life wouldn't appear so alluring on this occasion. Circumstances had changed profoundly, and the effect of the past was killing us.

Our inner cabin was designed for one person with enough spare room for an immobile corgi, but that was all. Graciously supplied by some obscure fund starved ministry of the UK to promote tourism, Reynaldo was given stateroom 4.045 (on deck 4 next to the laundry) at a ceremony involving Queen Elizabeth and the press. Needless to say, I was wiggling with enthusiasm for all of the attention I was receiving, but Reynaldo could only just manage to stand along side of me, holding my leash and foot stopping my wheels so that I wouldn't charge into the crowd to receive pets and treats and adulation. These few moments of celebrity were to be my last for a long time. After the press event, we were limousined to the pier where our ship awaited.

Reynaldo carried me and my wheels up the gangway with no difficulty as his luggage had been dealt with by someone belonging to the crew. We entered the two story

high lobby and immediately people were petting me and trying to speak with Reynaldo. Sadly, he could only be monosyllabic in his responses and so my chance for attention and perhaps a treat were cut short.

The fact that we were on a ship and not an airliner was a godsend for both of us. I would have been terrified of an airport and would have shivered with fear if I were placed in the hold of an airplane. Reynaldo also had no stomach for flying, though I don't think he was afraid except for the heart wrenching memories a flight would produce. The ever-present doom-cloud of what must have happened to Francine was rendering Reynaldo into a zombie-like state. The constant loop of Francine memories would keep the old, happy Reynaldo away for some time to come.

For me it was a little different. As I have told you too many times, my memory fleets from my brain like a mosquito in a hurricane. I was recollecting Francine only at dinner-time, walk time, and bedtime. Little twinges of Francine essence in the form of a recalled odor or the soft touch on my body by Reynaldo lifting me would flash through my thought processes with the speed of a spark. If only Reynaldo had my brain, he wouldn't suffer so much.

Another difference for me was the liberty extended to us by Cunard Ship Lines. I'm traveling in a cabin, not the kennel. Ordinarily this would be a pleasant plus because I'm with Reynaldo but, sadly, we couldn't be farther apart. Not my choice, obviously, Reynaldo simply can't function for two. His world is solitary for the time being and I'll just have to try to understand this. I realize that we are always alone in this life, but it was so nice when we were all alone together.

TO BOOF OR
NOT TO BOOF

It's 6:10 AM, a ridiculously late hour for me, and I'm boofing, he's sleeping. Boof-sleep, boof-sleep. Nothing is moving up there. I'll try barking. Bark-sleep bark-sleepy move, bark-Winnie be quiet, bark-he's sitting up now. Reynaldo sees me and I see him. We look at each other, Reynaldo in a fog but friendly. Me alert beyond all belief.

I need to go out doors and I need to eat. Two seemingly simple things but I can't do them without him. Reynaldo is now up and dressed in about five minutes, five minutes I really don't have because I really do need to go out doors.

He's picking me up and we are on our way downstairs to the kitchen where my chariot awaits. Once I'm secured we go around the side of the house and out to the street. This is just a quick utility walk and then it's back inside.

Nothing wrong with the way he leads, but he's no Francine. Francine was ALPHA for me and I really don't sense that energy from Reynaldo. He's affectionate and does everything Francine used to do for me but something is decidedly different. He sits for long periods of time doing nothing. I can sense unhappiness in him. There's no coffee smell, no reading of the newspaper, nor talk of politics or other morning chit-chat, just extreme quiet.

I'm unhappy too because even though I can't pin point this hollow feeling in me, it's due to the fact that I haven't seen, felt, heard, or smelled Francine for a long, long time. This is unbearable. No Francine, no alpha, no anchor in my life. I find myself whimpering sometimes, which isn't my style. Reynaldo must feel the same way. I've witnessed him crying, which upsets me no end. Francine is our world.

40

DOGSPLOITATION

Though I've observed Reynaldo moping around the house most days, half-heartedly working in the graphic studio and half-heartedly taking care of me, he did muster up some enthusiasm for one thing: marketing me. And once he did, boy did things change. With all the hoopla about my ordeal and the worldwide attention I receive to this day, he was advised by a lawyer friend to get going and not waste this opportunity to exploit the (my) situation.

As you might surmise, I've no idea what any of this is about, but I again can't help but take in all that happens around me and DOGSPEAK can't help but translate it. In terms of the marketing (or exploitation), there really wasn't any inconvenience other than some posing for photographers. The photography involved me walking in the neighborhood, standing on some white paper at the photographer's studio, eating some great food from a special (faux) "royal" bowl, and some interaction with Gus, my Saint Bernard friend.

The Gus session went well and when I did my customary growl at Gus, he responded as he should (a whimper and a cringe) and everyone in the room

applauded. Gus was delighted too because he got many treats for just being himself. Once we had a difficult moment because we had to keep the DOGSPEAK stereotactic cap on our heads for a long time. The problem was the usual one where Gus would shake it off, only this time people were trying to take a picture and of course that's exactly when he would lose the cap. The solution was to strap it on his head, which you can't do during a real DOGSPEAK retrieval because the pressure would be too great, but for the pictures a strap was fine. Gus looked particularly silly that way and we traded sympathetic glances. As much as we dogs love to be with humans, there are downsides.

The photographs were destined to promote a broad range of products such as a video game called Doggie Nights, a book bag, a Transformer action figure, raincoats (both human and dog), pajamas, sheets and blankets, a stuffed me with a working wheelchair (I actually speak in this one), and an entire laboratory with action figures including me, Gus, Reynaldo, Francine, and Lord Northridge.

Then there are the books: *The Kindness of Strangers* (as a graphic novel), *THE ADVENTURES OF OCEANDOG, Winnie and Gus: The Story of Lord Northridge's creation of DOGSPEAK,* and *Winnie Walks at Night (a mystery)*. As if that were not enough Winnie, a TV series called Winnie and the Queen was discussed for public broadcasting: the Queen and I solve murders and

recruit the entire Queen's Corgi and Dorgi menagerie to surround, pounce and pummel villains of all types.

But the biggest project was the animated movie of The Kindness of Strangers. It documents the whole ordeal, pretty much as you have just read it, which means, of course, retelling of the loss of Francine. This was particularly tough on Reynaldo and caused a lapse of several months before he completed the screenplay for it.

If I were a person I could get pretty rapped up in myself over all of this, but, dare I say it again, as a dog none of this registers at all. It is just a series of unrelated events without sequence or consequence to me other than meeting new people who are exceedingly nice to me.

But there seems to be an overall feeling in the back of my mind about these events and about Reynaldo and his relationship to me. I'll call it a memory ache. Before the lawyer spoke to him about the Winnie projects, Reynaldo was only partially there for me. And, I hate to say it, but Francine had become a dim memory. Her absence left a feeling of incompleteness about everything that happens throughout the day and a lack in everything Reynaldo does for me. That's my memory ache.

But Reynaldo has become my primary and, half-hearted or not, he does do all of the necessary things I require of a primary. I do feel love from him. And maybe I wasn't all there either because my physical situation has taken a turn for the worse. My front legs are weakening.

My wheelchair has provisions for the attachment of front wheels but that is no consolation. I have to stay where I'm put; I can't crawl around like I use to do. I guess I require a lot more attention. But since the marketing of the various Winnie projects, especially writing it all out for the animation, Reynaldo seems much happier to oblige.

We go for walks four or five times a day. He stops and talks to neighbors. I get plenty of treats and he massages me for a good half-hour straight daily. My massages, which we do on the bedroom floor while watching old movies on the TV, are particularly soothing because Reynaldo is touching me in ways that take away some arthritis pain. He even flexes my wrists and toes. When he massages the back of my neck it reminds me of my puppy days when Hanna, my mother, would pick me up with her mouth, by the back of the neck, and move me around in the big cardboard box I was born in.

After massage I get my belly combed, which means I'm on my back and I close my eyes, put my face and nose against Reynaldo's leg and sleep and dream. Many times this dream is of walks in the neighborhood with Francine, maybe picking up an apple from the sidewalk in front of our neighbor's apple tree and carrying one in my mouth for the whole walk. See, there are memories of a sort buried away in the recesses of my moment-to-moment mind. Francine, Reynaldo, Shorty, Gus, Lord Northridge, all the neighbors and their dogs,

they're all there somewhere. The treats, the dinners, the massages, my wheelchair, all in my mind, all connected somehow into one great big extravaganza of misty memory and feeling. The scarier moments are all gone, but those big events, the trip to England, Dr. Cougar and Nurse Robin, Queen Elizabeth and Simon Pearson, Vulcan, and the others, are still there and included in my joy of living.

I am a moment-to-moment being, yes, with each moment held together by this glue of instinctual memories prodded along by this and that. When I think back along this memory trail and feel, in a vague way of course, sensations of what has occurred in my years of living, I don't have a feeling of good (or bad) luck, privilege or entitlement, just the heavenly now of well-being and comfort. And every morning when I wake up at 5:20AM it is with nothing but shear happiness that I boof at Reynaldo to wake him up too. I'm sure we share this feeling.

The bedroom is dark and cozy but for the light of the television. Reynaldo's leg shifts a tiny bit moving my head ever so slightly and I become aware of the TV. A woman's voice in the movie he's watching sounds remarkably like a voice from our past. A mental prodding. I awaken more and look up at Reynaldo; he looks down at me, and I swear, not forgetting the limitations my flaps permit, we both smile.

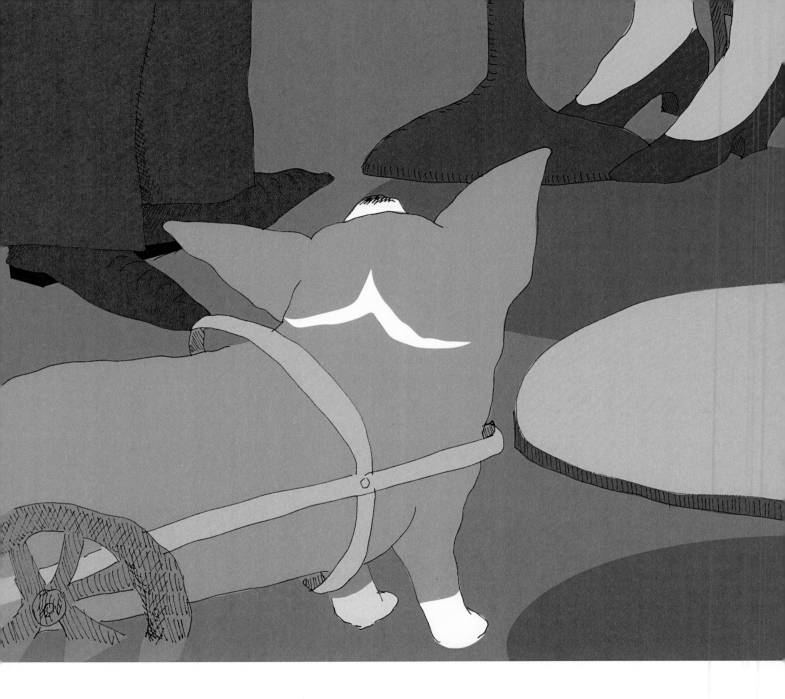

EPILOGUE

Winnie's front legs have improved with therapy and massage allowing her to crawl about the house at will. Reynaldo and Winnie have lived together, happily, for a year and a half since the crash.

Recently Reynaldo decided to take Winnie to Paris, and while there they renewed their relationship with Francine quite by chance. As he and Winnie were strolling along Place Vendome, they both recognized a voice at a nearby table from a sidewalk café. The voice belonged to Francine.

Though she didn't recognize either of them, she was friendly and happy to speak with them. She had a prominent scar and indentation on her forehead and used a cane, but otherwise looked, sounded, and smelled exactly as they remembered her.

Suffering from total amnesia, she had started a new life in France as a painter. Minutes after having been told of her past life with Reynaldo and Winnie and sharing their joy of this chance reunion, she smiled politely, looked from Reynaldo and then down to Winnie and said, "Please refresh my memory. Who are you two again?"

what Dogspeak is and isn't

You have just read the product of DOGSPEAK, the animal to human translation program by Lord David Northridge in collaboration with Reynaldo Dumont.

My part is simple enough. They attach surface electrodes to my head using a stereotactic cap with specially fitted ear openings to a computer running DOGSPEAK 1.0.

As a dog, my thoughts are without any language at all, so DOGSPEAK retrieves them utilizing Lord Northridge's patented surface electrode fMRI technology, and through sentiment analysis translates the impulses into something that flows like human written language with the help of thesauruses, dictionaries, and encyclopedias. Reynaldo has input into the program a detailed profile covering both my physical and mental attributes to help round out the translations. These translations are referred to as retrievals and are printed out in raw prose, a prose that is somewhat less flowing than what you are now reading.

Amazing as DOGSPEAK is, it's not perfect. For one thing, it doesn't make speech a possibility. Speech is a purely human miracle. For another, my thoughts and memories are not always retrieved in chronological order.

DOGSPEAK fills in a lot of details that aren't really part of my thinking and, on the whole, lacks metaphorical ability, giving a rather dry accounting of my thoughts and sensual memories, though it does a wonderful job of elaborating on my emotions, which is why what you've read may give the impression of coming from a human. But it didn't!

Made in the USA
San Bernardino, CA
24 June 2017